Emma's American Chinese New Year

AMY MEADOWS

Illustrations by
Soon Kwong Teo

Emma's American Chinese New Year
All Rights Reserved.
Copyright © 2012 Amy Meadows
v2.0

Cover and Interior Illustrations by Soon Kwong Teo.
Cover and Interior Illustrations © 2012 Outskirts Press, Inc. All rights reserved - used with permission.

Outskirts Press, Inc.
http://www.outskirtspress.com

ISBN: 978-1-4327-8694-6

Library of Congress Control Number: 2012902578

Outskirts Press and the "OP" logo are trademarks belonging to Outskirts Press, Inc.

PRINTED IN THE UNITED STATES OF AMERICA

This book belongs to:

For Briana and Noah

It is time to celebrate the New Year in China –
the country where I was born!
They are welcoming spring with
lanterns and lions and so much more.

I live in America now
because Mommy and Daddy adopted me.
But the holiday is still special,
and my whole family agrees.

When the first two months of the year
come around, we get ready to have some fun.
We decorate the house and bake moon cakes –
there is just so much to be done.

I love to make Chinese lanterns
from colored paper and ribbons.
Mommy hangs them across the fireplace
as soon as I have finished them.

We also like to eat oranges
because the New Year will surely be sweet.
They are so juicy and delicious –
their taste just can't be beat.

And to make sure that good luck finds me,
a red envelope I receive
with dollar bills inside of it –
sometimes as many as three!

Then my favorite day arrives
when we all gather together
to celebrate the Lunar New Year
at the local cultural center.

My aunt and uncle come with us –
just like Grandma and Grandpa do.
They bring my cousin Max with them –
he has been joining us since he was two.

Every year I make sure to wear
a brand new red qipao dress.
It is the color of luck in China,
and in it I feel like a princess.

When we get to the cultural center,
it is true that I often see
little girls in qipao dresses
who look very much like me!

I love to hear the Chinese drums
as soon as we walk in the door.
The music is loud and exciting,
and it makes my heart want to soar!

The drummers' hands move so quickly
that the music sounds like thunder.
They play together in unison,
and to watch them is really a wonder!

I always wait for the dancers
who wave feathered fans in the air.
They wear brightly colored costumes
and flowers in their hair.

They whirl, they twirl, they spin and they sway
to a traditional Chinese melody.
And when they finish we clap and cheer
for the great talent that we see.

Max wants to be a Kung Fu artist
like the ones we watch each year.
When they get ready to come on stage,
he starts grinning from ear to ear.

They jump, they leap, they twist and they kick –
it is quite a sight to see.
And when they swing big shiny swords,
I can tell it is not easy!

The excitement builds when we head outside
to the parking lot late in the day.
We know who is coming and no one can wait
for the lion to come out and play.

His head is so big and furry –
I want to reach out and pet it!
And when he dances to the cymbals and drums,
it is always a really big hit!

Then the dragon follows the lion
to do his own special dance.
He brings us all good luck and success
as soon as he makes his entrance.

The dragon is long and colorful,
and he looks like he is flying on air.
When he quickly dips down and sweeps around,
it is a show that's beyond compare!

As the celebration comes to an end,
we head out for a yummy meal.
We go to our favorite Chinese restaurant,
which we visit year after year.

We dine on dumplings, spring rolls and fish,
and we all enjoy it so.
To have a long life, we also eat noodles
like my ancestors did long ago.

The fortune cookies arrive at the end,
and we crack them open with glee.
Every one has a special message inside
that makes each of us very happy!

Then it is time to say "Gung Hay Fat Choy!"
because the New Year is finally here.
It means so much for me to celebrate
with the family I hold so dear.

Chinese New Year will always be
an important part of my life.
Mommy and Daddy say they'll make sure of it
because I am the apple of their eye!

Gung Hay Fat Choy!

Xin Nian Kuai Le!

新年快樂

Happy New Year!

CPSIA information can be obtained
at www.ICGtesting.com
Printed in the USA
LVIC06n1002190114
370037LV00008B/44

9 781432 786946